To Live a Truer Life

A Story of the Hopedale Community

Written by Lynn Gordon Hughes
Illustrated by Lindro

Blackstone Editions
Providence

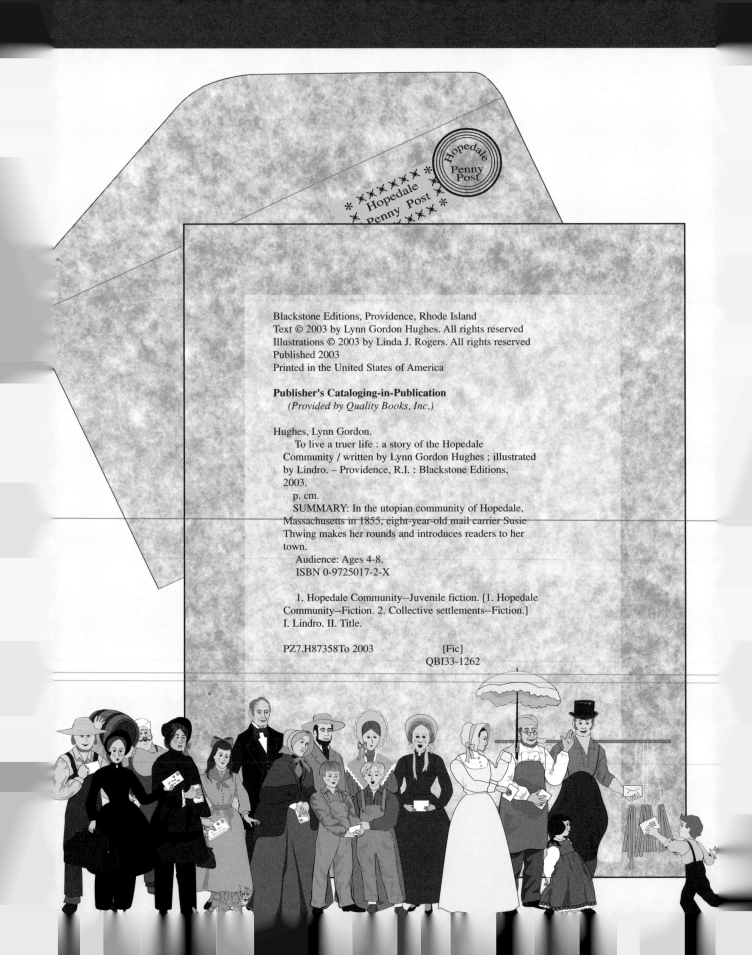

Blackstone Editions, Providence, Rhode Island
Published 2003
Printed in the United States of America

Publisher's Cataloging-in-Publication
  (Provided by Quality Books, Inc.)

Hughes, Lynn Gordon.
    To live a truer life : a story of the Hopedale
Community / written by Lynn Gordon Hughes ; illustrated
by Lindro. – Providence, R.I. : Blackstone Editions,
2003.
    p. cm.
    SUMMARY: In the utopian community of Hopedale,
Massachusetts in 1855, eight-year-old mail carrier Susie
Thwing makes her rounds and introduces readers to her
town.
    Audience: Ages 4-8.
    ISBN 0-9725017-2-X

    1. Hopedale Community--Juvenile fiction. [1. Hopedale
Community--Fiction. 2. Collective settlements--Fiction.]
I. Lindro. II. Title.

PZ7.H87358To 2003   [Fic]
                             QBI33-1262

To Amy G. Remensnyder
scholar, teacher, peacemaker
&. Lynn Gordon Hughes

To my children, George, Christina,
Alex... and especially for my
grandson, Cody Vermeulen,
helper, co-artist and best critic.
&. Lindro

Susie's Hopedale

to Mendon

Freedom Street

to Milford

Red Shop

School

Johnson

Woods

Path to Milford

Chapel Street

Workshops

Water Street

Social Street

Old House

High Street

Woods

Union Street

Main Street

Ballou

Peace Street

Thwing

Humphrey

Hope Street

Beal

The Field

Meadow Lane

To the Pine Grove and South Milford

ere comes the mail! I've been busy weeding the garden – and eating a few nice ripe strawberries – but I jump up and wipe the dirt off my hands when I see Mr. Southwick coming down the street with the mail bag. Mr. Southwick is the express driver. Twice a day, except on Sunday, he drives the stage coach from Hopedale to Milford and back to Hopedale. In Milford, he has an important job to do – he takes the mail from Hopedale to the post office and picks up the mail for everyone in Hopedale.

"Evening, Susie!" calls Mr. Southwick. "Plenty of mail today."

"Yes, and I'm going to deliver it all," I answer. "Anna is busy studying for the examinations, so mother said I could take her route today."

H opedale is too small to have a real post office, but it's too far for
everyone to go to Milford to get their mail. That's why we have the
Hopedale Penny Post. We have special Hopedale stamps, too. They are
pink and say HOPEDALE PENNY POST.

My mother is the postmistress. If anyone in Hopedale has a letter to mail,
they give it to my mother or drop it in a box in our woodshed. My father cut
a hole in the wall of the woodshed and put up a sign saying LETTER BOX.

My sister Anna and I are the mail carriers. When Mr. Southwick comes
back from Milford with the letters and newspapers, Anna and I deliver them.
Usually Anna takes the north end of town and I take the south. But our
school examinations are next week, and Anna is working hard to get ready.

Anna is in the first class, so she has to do all kinds of hard things, like Geography, and Physiology, and parts of speech and percents and square roots. Right now she is worrying about the Geography examination. She might be called on to draw a map of Europe or South America, with all the cities and rivers and everything, without even looking at a book. I'm in the third class. We do reading and arithmetic, and we show the examiners our compositions and our drawings. But we don't worry about examinations the way the first class students do.

I don't mind doing Anna's route today, because it's nice and warm, and it's still light even though it's after seven in the evening. In the winter I have to wear a hood, and heavy boots, and leather mittens that make it hard to get the letters out of the mail bag. I carry a lantern with glass all around to keep the wind from blowing the lamp out.

I have three letters and three newspapers for Mr. Adin Ballou. Mr. Ballou is a very important man – I guess he is the most important person in Hopedale. If not for Mr. Ballou, there wouldn't even be any Hopedale. It was his idea to start a new town, a place for people who want to live in a special way. We are called Non-Resistants.

At school we talk a lot about what it means to be a Non-Resistant. *Resist* means *fight back*. Non-Resistant means we don't fight back – no matter what! Everyone who lives in Hopedale has to promise never to kill, hurt, or hate anybody, even their worst enemy.

We made up a dialogue about this at school, and two of the boys acted it out. One of the boys pretended to be a Non-Resistant called "Billy." Billy talked to another boy called "George," who thought Non-Resistants were silly. The dialogue went something like this:

GEORGE: My father told me, if anyone hits me, to hit back just as hard, no matter how big the other fellow is.

BILLY: My mother told me to be kind and forgiving, even though most people do as your father tells you. She says she has tried both ways, and likes this best.

GEORGE: Your mother is a woman, and my father is a man.

BILLY: That doesn't matter. When Jesus said, "Blessed are the peacemakers," he didn't mean to bless only the women.

GEORGE: My father says the world is not prepared to live so.

BILLY: If everyone waits for it to be prepared, no one will ever begin. Here is a puzzle for you, George: if everyone waits for someone else to begin, how long will it be before the world is perfect? Good-bye; mother is calling me. (He leaves)

GEORGE: Maybe Billy is not so silly after all. Maybe I am the silly one.

I turn off Main Street to deliver some letters and newspapers to my uncle, Mr. George Draper. On the way I pass the Old House. It is more than 150 years old. George Washington visited it once, and it was an old house even then.

Some people call it the Elder Jones House because it was built by a man named John Jones (my great, great, great grandfather). There was no town here then, just woods, and Indians, and wolves and bears.

When Mr. Ballou started Hopedale, the Old House was the only house here. So when people came to Hopedale, they all moved into the Old House. More and more people came, until there were 45 people living in one old house. You can imagine how crowded it was!

The first to move in were the Lillie family – Sybil, Henry, Sarah, and Lucy Lillie and their parents. I wasn't born then, but Sarah Lillie told me all about it. She used to look after me when I was little, and I loved to hear her tell stories about the old days.

Sarah and Lucy shared a little bed that pulled out from under their parents' bed. The older children all slept in the attic, boys in one room and girls in the other. There was another attic where people kept all the things that wouldn't fit in their rooms.

When the house got too noisy, Sarah used to go into that attic to get some peace and quiet. There was a mother cat up there who let Sarah play with her kittens.

$\mathcal{E}$veryone ate together in the big dining room. One of the men was a baker. He baked bread, pies, beans, and gingerbread for everybody. Mrs. Ballou and my aunt Anna Draper were in charge of the rest of the cooking.

S ometimes I think it would be fun to live in a big old house like that — it would be like Thanksgiving every day! But other times I'm glad I live in a quiet little house.

S ometimes it got too noisy for Mr. Ballou, so he made up rhymes to help
the children remember to be quiet. Here is one that Sarah taught me:

I'll think and take care how I stamp, stamp, stamp

When I traverse the rooms, above or below.

And never disturb, with a wild horse tramp tramp,

The feelings of those to whom noise is a woe.

When Sarah went to school back in the Old House days, Mr. Ballou was the teacher. I think I would be a little bit afraid if Mr. Ballou was my teacher.

Sarah told me how sorry she felt when he scolded her because she and another little girl made a playhouse under his desk. And once she was in terrible disgrace for fighting in school – which is something a good Non-Resistant should never do.

*T*his big building is where I go to school. My teacher is called Mrs. Abbie. Her name is really Mrs. Abbie Ballou Heywood, but we call her Mrs. Abbie because we are so fond of her. Once we had to write a composition on "My Wish," and Willie Fish wished that he might live to be a hundred years old and go to Mrs. Abbie's school every day of his life.

On Sundays everyone goes to the schoolhouse, because it is also the chapel. We have Sunday School in the morning and church services in the afternoon. The bell in the clock tower rings when it is time for school or church. I am specially proud of the clock because my father made it.

Children all, both young and old,
With your eyes you now behold
Hung with fruits, the Christmas Tree.

Dollies, rosy-cheeked and fair,
Box and bag, and cap and cape
Gifts of every size and shape

Such a smiling evergreen
As I think was never seen!

At Christmas time, we have our Christmas Festival in the schoolhouse. The school room is filled with evergreen wreaths trimmed with ribbons, and looks so beautiful. We always start the festival with a school exhibition. I love to sing and recite! One year I recited a piece called "A Mother's Love." Last Christmas I did an exciting one called "A Stormy Night."

After the exhibition we all get out our picnic baskets and share apples, cake, popcorn, and other good things. After we eat, there are more songs and recitations. Then two of the big boys draw the curtain, and at last we see the tree, with gifts for everyone hanging from the branches.

O ver here are some of our Hopedale workshops. In these shops people
make furniture, boxes, boots and shoes, books and newspapers, soap,
candles, and parts for machines. I don't think I would like to work in a
shop. If I wasn't a mail carrier, I think I would like to look after the horses or
work in the nursery taking care of trees and plants.

The top floor of one of the shops is a big open hall. Every Saturday night (that's tonight!) we have dances here. Men, women, and children all dance together. We do square dances and contra dances. The children get to stay up until 9:30 on dancing night. On other nights we have to be at home by 8:00.

𝓘 have a letter to deliver to Mrs. Johnson way out at the end of Chapel Street, and one for Mr. Beal, the shoemaker. To get to Mr. Beal's house, I go by High Street. We call it a street, but it is really just a footpath. Today it still has some muddy puddles left from yesterday's rain. I'm glad I'm not wearing a long dress, or it would be trailing in the mud.

Mrs. Fish, our sewing teacher, says that's why long skirts are silly. She says girls can wear short skirts, so why not grown women? Mrs. Fish likes to wear a Bloomer Dress. It has a short skirt with pants underneath, like my pantalets. Many women in Hopedale wear them for work, but Mrs. Fish wears hers even to church.

Near Mr. Beal's house is a field filled with wildflowers and berry bushes. On the first of May we picked flowers there to make May baskets, bouquets, and a wreath for the Queen of the May. Lizzie Humphrey was Queen of the May. Lizzie is so beautiful and she draws beautiful pictures, too. At the May Festival all the children carried bouquets and sang,

Flowers! Flowers! Come forth, 'tis Spring!

Stars of the hills, the woods, and the dells,

Fair valley-lilies, come forth and ring

In your green turrets your silvery bells.

D own the path from the wildflower field is the pine grove where we hold our Anti-Slavery Celebration every year on the first of August. The first of August is a happy day because that is the day the slaves were freed in the British West India islands. All of us hope and pray that the slaves will soon be freed in the United States.

Sometimes escaped slaves stay with us at Hopedale. Most of them don't stay very long. They are on their way to Canada, where there is no slavery. But sometimes they stay a long time. There was a family with two children who stayed in Hopedale for a whole year. The oldest girl went to school with us and learned to read and write.

Last summer we had a giant celebration – my father said there must have been about a thousand people there! We listened to a lot of speeches. One was by a man with long hair and a long beard. He said he would never cut his hair until the slaves were free.

The best speech of all was by a woman named Sojourner Truth, who used to be a slave. She told us about her life in slavery. It made Anna cry, and it made me so angry that I almost forgot about being a Non-Resistant. Then she told us that white people were nice and clean on the outside, but her job was to make them clean inside. "I think they need a good deal of scrubbing, though!" she said, which made us laugh. At the end of the day we sang Anti-Slavery songs, and everyone shouted,

**"Slavery nowhere but Liberty everywhere,
throughout our country and throughout the world!"**

O n the other side of the field is the house of Dr. Emily Gay. Dr. Emily is not home, so I leave her letters under her door and go on to Mr. Hatch's house. I know Mr. Hatch very well because he leads our singing school. He gives me two letters to put in the mail bag. "That will be three cents, please," I say, and give him two pink stamps.

When I come out of Mr. Hatch's house, I see Dr. Emily hurrying down Main Street. She is wearing a Bloomer (she says they are good for the health) and carrying her medicine chest.

I have only one letter left to deliver. It is for Mr. Humphrey, Lizzie Humphrey's father. The Humphreys live just down the street from us, so I am almost home.

Mr. and Mrs. Humphrey are known in Hopedale for being specially kind and generous. Whenever a poor and hungry stranger comes to town, he is sure of getting a meal and a place to stay at the Humphreys' house.

One night, Lizzie Humphrey was in bed when she heard strange noises in the house. She told her parents, and they went to look. A man was hiding under the sofa in the parlor, with just his feet sticking out. Near him on the floor was a bag filled with things taken from their dining room. Lizzie had caught a burglar!

Lizzie ran to get Mr. Ballou, my father, my uncle Ebenezer, and some of the other neighbors. When they got to the Humphreys' house, they wondered what to do. Non-Resistants don't believe in hurting anyone, not even a burglar. Finally they all went into the parlor. One held a lamp while four others lifted the sofa off the man.

*T*hey saw that the burglar was a poor man who had come to the house earlier for some food and medicine.

"What are you doing here?" asked Mr. Humphrey.

The man said that he had no home, no work, and no food. "I thought if I stole something, I would get sent to a place where they would feed me," he said.

"We will feed you," said Mr. Humphrey. "You don't need to steal anything." So the man stayed with them until they found him a place to live.

Later someone asked Mrs. Humphrey, "Didn't you feel real provoked with that man, to come back to rob you after you tried to help him?" But Mrs. Humphrey just laughed. "Why, no," she said. "I felt as if I wanted to take him right in my arms."

My last letter is delivered, and I'm home in time for the dancing. Soon Anna and my parents and I will walk up Main Street to the big red shop by the pond. On the way we will meet our friends and neighbors, all going to the same place. We will climb the rickety stairs to the dancing hall. Then the music will begin. We always have a fiddler, and sometimes other instruments like the flute, clarinet, and accordion. Just before we leave, we will all sing together.

We have come from various quarters.
Both parents, sons and daughters,
We have come from various quarters
To live a truer life.
And here we stand, joined heart and hand,
And here we hope to win the day,
Oppose who will, oppose who may,
And here we hope to win the day
And live a truer life.

To Live a Truer Life
by Daniel S. Whitney

We have come from various quarters,
Both parents, sons, and daughters,
We have come from various quarters
To live a truer life.
And here we stand, joined heart and hand,
And here we hope to win the day,
Oppose who will, oppose who may;
And here we hope to win the day
And live a truer life.

We've met with many trials,
Have had some self-denials,
We've met with many trials
In founding here a home.
Yet here we stand, joined heart and hand,
And here we mean to conquer sin,
Our foes without and foes within;
Then Heaven on earth will here begin
For humble souls a home.

Now all our prospects brighten,
Experience doth enlighten,
Small matters do not frighten,
In order we progress.
We labor all, both great and small;
All energies uniting,
Makes labor more inviting,
Activity delighting
Right onward now we press.

The Hopedale Community

All of the people and places mentioned in *To Live a Truer Life* are real. We have done our best to portray them as accurately as possible, in both the words and the pictures. No effort to re-create the past is ever completely successful, but we trust we have captured something of the spirit of community life.

The Hopedale Community was established in 1841 by Adin and Lucy Ballou, Ebenezer and Anna Draper, and others who were interested in developing a new way of living, based on their understanding of the teachings of Jesus and the will of God. They called themselves "Practical Christians" because they intended to put their religion into practice in their daily life.

The Practical Christians believed in a radical form of non-violence called Christian Non-Resistance, which rejected not only war and capital punishment, but all authority based on force. Therefore, they did not vote or participate in government, or make use of police or courts. In an era when even short periods of illness or unemployment could leave families destitute, they guaranteed jobs for all able-bodied members, and loving care for those unable to work. At a time when the anti-slavery cause was just beginning to gather momentum, and the women's rights movement still lay in the future, the Hopedale constitution proclaimed that all members "shall stand on a footing of personal equality, irrespective of sex, color, occupation, wealth, rank, or any other natural or adventitious peculiarity." They put their principles to the test by sheltering escaping slaves and by extending their charity even to a burglar who came to rob them.

The Hopedale Community lasted for fifteen years, far longer than most experiments of this kind. It came to an end, quite suddenly, in the spring of 1856. Ebenezer Draper's brother George, who had recently joined the community, persuaded his brother to join him in withdrawing their assets from the common treasury, claiming that the community was not using sound accounting practices. Another factor undoubtedly was that an opportunity had recently opened for the brothers to expand their business – but only if they could hire more workers and put more of the profits into the business, instead of into the community. As the brothers owned the majority of the shares, the community collapsed without their support. The Draper Corporation remained a vital presence in the town of Hopedale until the 1970s.

Those familiar with the history of Hopedale can work out that the story takes place in the summer of 1855, when our narrator Susan Thwing was eight years old. The Hopedale Penny Post, the living arrangements in the Old House, the community festivals, the encounter with the burglar, and many other details are part of the historical record. Even Susan's voice – cheery, outgoing, proud of her town and eager to share it with others – is not entirely our invention. All of these qualities are to be found in the memoir of her childhood which she wrote when she was in her sixties.

Susan lived in Hopedale for the rest of her life. In 1867 she married James Whitney, Adin Ballou performing the ceremony. Susan and James had three children: Mabel; Almon, named for Susan's father; and Anna, named for her sister. In his *History of the Town of Milford* (Hopedale was part of Milford until 1886), Adin Ballou tells us that the little girl who loved to sing and recite grew up to be "an excellent contralto singer, and is much employed in church choirs, at funerals, and on other occasions."

Looking back on the Community in later years, Susan wrote, "Surely they hitched their wagon to a star – and though it fell to earth, it left a pathway so bright that it still points the way to perfection."

Acknowledgements

Anyone writing about the Hopedale Community owes a great debt to the people of the community who took the trouble to record their stories for the benefit of future generations. The most important source of the information in *To Live a Truer Life* is the set of memoirs collected by the Hopedale Ladies' Sewing Circle and Branch Alliance, published as *Hopedale Reminiscences* in 1910. The contributors included Abbie Ballou Heywood, then aged eighty-one, along with eight women and one man who had been children at Hopedale over a half-century before. Of particular importance are "The Old House of Hopedale" by Sarah Lillie Daniels, "The Post Office" and "The Burglary" by Susan Thwing Whitney, and "Anti-Slavery and Other Visitors to the Community" by Anna Thwing Field. Another important source is the community newspaper, the *Practical Christian*. The school examinations, the dialogue on non-resistance, the program of the Christmas and May Festivals, Margaret Fish's views on dress, and Sojourner Truth's speech, all came from the *Practical Christian*. The most complete story of the community's life is in Adin Ballou's *History of the Hopedale Community*.

The Bancroft Memorial Library in Hopedale has served for generations as the keeper of the Community's archives. Visitors to the library can read the *Practical Christian* and see Adin Ballou's desk. The pictures of Adin Ballou, Dr. Emily Gay, Mr. and Mrs. Humphrey, the Old House, and the Hopedale shops are all based on originals in the library's collections. We thank Hopedale historians Elaine and Daniel Malloy and Alan J. Ryan for their helpful book, *Hopedale* (Images of America, 2002), and for answering our questions about the complicated history of the Old House and the Red Shop.

This book started life as a project for a graduate seminar in the History Department at Brown University, in which students were encouraged to explore alternative methods of presenting historical information: historical fiction, personal essays, dramatic monologues, web sites, even a computer game. I thank Professor Amy Remensnyder and classmates Regine Heberlein, Lindsay Kelley, and Shih-Chieu Su for the combination of rigorous criticism and perfect mutual trust that called forth from each of us work that we had not previously known we could do.

Lynn Gordon Hughes

This book has been made possible in part through the funding of the New York State Convention of Universalists and the Unitarian Sunday School Society.